GAUTAM'S GOODBYE

WRITTEN AND ILLUSTRATED BY ARUNA KHANZADA

For all the memories.

First published in the United Kingdom in 2024 by Aruna Khanzada
www.myredbag.uk

Text © Aruna Khanzada 2024
Illustrations © Aruna Khanzada 2024

P-ISBN: 978-1-9164962-5-5

On a crisp spring night,
when the moon was full and bright,
Gautam the little elephant was born.

1

Under the mulberry tree
Gautam grew tall and strong.
He lived there with
BaBoo the elephant, MooMa the cow,
Saveeta the tortoise and Rekha the rabbit.

In the summer,
Gautam played in the
flower meadow.

He ate sweet and juicy mulberries.

and he splish-splashed in the river
with Saveeta and Rekha.

4

Gautam thought life would always be
as warm and sunny as summer.

But life does not stand still.
Things began to change.

"MooMa," said Gautam,
"The mulberries have gone.
The flowers are wilting.
The leaves are not green anymore."

WHY?

"Life is like a circle," said MooMa.
"The moon waxes and wanes. Seasons change.
Summer is ending and autumn is coming.

Life does not stand still but your memories will."

7

"BaBoo, tell the leaves
not to fall.
Tell the flowers not to wilt.
Tell the mulberries to come back."

8

"Seasons change," said Baboo.
Autumn is here now and winter is on its way."

"The leaves will fall.
It will feel cold and bare for a time.
Then spring and summer will be here again.

Life does not stand still
but your memories will."

9

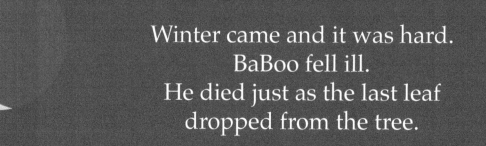

Winter came and it was hard.
BaBoo fell ill.
He died just as the last leaf
dropped from the tree.

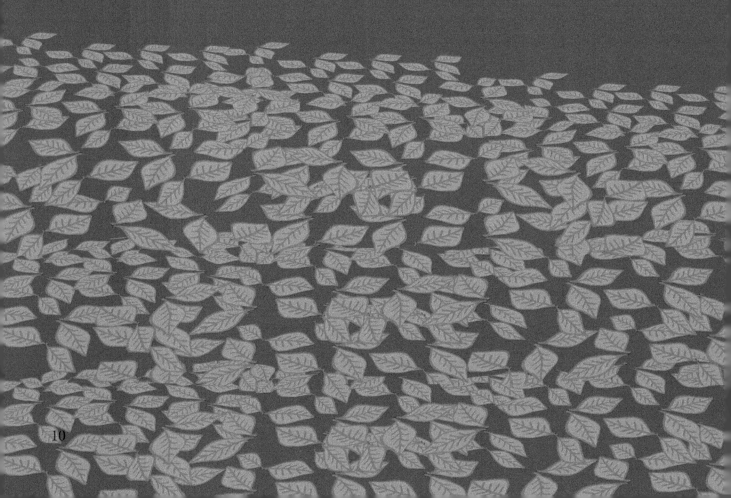

Gautam missed BaBoo so much it hurt.
Some times he thought he could see him in the snow.

Some times he thought he could see him in the rain.

Some times Gautam felt
SAD.

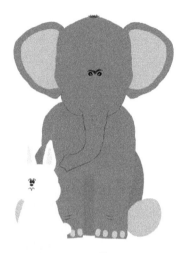

Some times Gautam got
MAD.

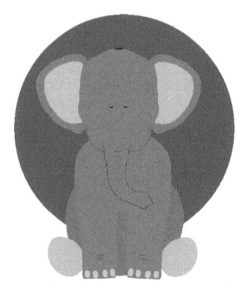

Some times Gautam just felt so
BAD.

"It is okay to feel
sad, mad or bad.
They are feelings
just like being
happy or glad.

Don't hide your feelings
and you will find
things will get better.
Just give it time,"
said MooMa

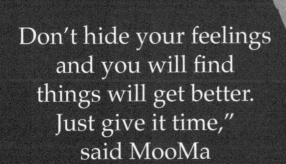

Spring came again.

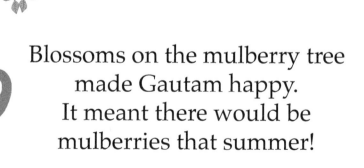

Blossoms on the mulberry tree
made Gautam happy.
It meant there would be
mulberries that summer!

Gautam remembered
BaBoo telling him
life does not stand still.

Gautam thought about the moon waxing and waning. From full moon to new moon and then back again. Life feels like that sometimes........

third quarter

waning crescent

waning gibbous

new moon

full moon

waxing crescent

first quarter

waxing gibbous

18

Gautam thought about how the seasons change. From spring to summer, then autumn to winter. Life feels like that sometimes too ....

When the grass grew green
and the flowers bloomed again,
20 Gautam felt much happier but he still missed BaBoo.

Everyone was glad summer was here
and they remembered the happy days
with BaBoo in the meadow.

22

The mulberries were ripe in summer.
Gautam was sad BaBoo was not there but
he was glad
to be eating juicy mulberries.

23

Autumn came again.
Gautam knew winter
was on its way.

Nothing can stop
the seasons changing.

The moon will wax and wane,
The leaves will fall and come back in spring.
BaBoo would never come back but Gautam knows:

Life will not stand still but his memories will.

Has someone special you know died?
Write down some memories of this person.

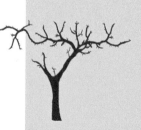

Make a memory box of photos and things to
remember the special moments.

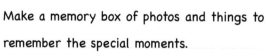

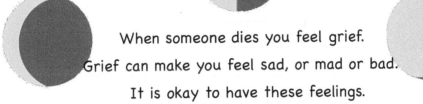

When someone dies you feel grief.

Grief can make you feel sad, or mad or bad.

It is okay to have these feelings.

Tick the boxes that you think might help you when you feel upset:

- ☐ Go outside and shout at the top of your voice.
- ☐ Do some messy painting.
- ☐ Play a sport you like as hard as you can.
- ☐ Cry if you want to!
- ☐ Find a quiet space to chill.
- ☐ If you are mad, get a cushion and punch it!
- ☐ Ask someone close to you for a cuddle.
- ☐ Run like the wind in a safe space.

Write down what else you think might help you:

Milton Keynes UK
Ingram Content Group UK Ltd.
UKHW021909180424
441304UK00003B/18